Babri is much like any other young tiger his age: curious, carefree, playful—full of life and energy and daring. Is it any wonder that he forgets his wise mother's counsel and wanders off into the jungle during naptime one day? What follows for Babri is a series of delightful, sometimes scary adventures that satisfy his curiosity—for the time being—leaving him exhilarated, bewildered, hungry, tired, and homesick for his mother and the fern glade where they live.

The artwork of Fahimeh Amiri is exquisite, enchanting, exotic. These illustrations inspired James Jacobs to craft an imaginative, lovable story to please youngsters of all ages. The text and artwork combine to impart an oriental flavor, using subtle yet charming images to underscore Babri's age-old quest for knowledge and experience.

Babri

Babri

Adapted by James Jacobs
from an illustrated story
by Fahimeh Amiri

GIBBS·SMITH
P
PUBLISHER

First edition
97 96 95 94   10 9 8 7 6 5 4 3 2 1

This is a Peregrine Smith Book, published by
Gibbs Smith, Publisher
P.O. Box 667
Layton, UT 84041

Printed and bound in China

Library of Congress Cataloging-in-Publication Data

Jacobs, James, 1945–
     Babri / adapted by James Jacobs from an
illustrated story by Fahimeh Amiri.
          p.   cm.
     Summary: A curious young tiger learns some
important lessons about life when, disregarding his
mother's warnings, he sets out to explore the jungle.
     ISBN 0-87905-622-3
     [1. Tigers—Fiction. 2. Jungles—Fiction.
3. Conduct of life—Fiction.] I. Amiri, Fahimeh, 1947– ill.
II. Title.
PZ7.J15235Bab   1994
[E]—dc20   94-11762
                                                   CIP
                                                    AC

This book is dedicated with the utmost appreciation to
Richard Tice
whose experience was invaluable
in the early development of this story,
and to
my beloved family
whose heartwarming support
made this book possible.
– F A –

To My Lights
Linda
Amy, Christian, Michael,
Andrew, Elizabeth, Jonathan,
Daniel and Matthew

– J J –

*B*abri and his mother lived in a small fern glade at the edge of the jungle. She knew the ways of the jungle and often told Babri, "My young child, whom I love more than sunshine, never go into the jungle alone." And Babri always replied, "Yes, Mother."

But Babri wondered about the jungle and about other things. Lately his mother had begun calling him "my why child" because he asked so many questions: "Why are ferns so soft?" "Why am I thirsty sometimes and sometimes not?" "Why do clouds change shape?"

Every afternoon was naptime, which Babri hated. This day he asked, again, "Why must I nap?"

"Oh, my why child, whom I love more than food and water, a nap is the way of things." She then smoothed his fur with her long tongue, closed her eyes, and began her soft sleeping purr.

But Babri closed only one eye, and because of that, he saw Mouse run right by his paw and straight into the jungle.

*W*hy do mice always run? Babri wondered. Easing himself from his sleeping mother, he ran after Mouse. With only a quick thought about entering the jungle, he shortly stumbled onto a family of mice. They scattered and Babri pounced, catching one by the tail.

"Why do mice always scurry? Tell me quickly, and I'll let you go," said Babri.

"We have little choice but to use our legs, for we have no long claws, no sharp teeth, and no bulging muscles," said Mouse. "Those who can't fight must flee. That is the way of things for mice."

Satisfied, Babri lifted his paw and watched Mouse scamper to safety.

*B*abri looked around and realized he was in the jungle for the first time in his life. By himself. Alone. But he could still see the fern glade where his mother was sleeping.

Suddenly, something smacked onto the ground right next to him. Babri looked up to see Squirrel running along a broad tree limb. Reaching the tip, Squirrel sprang to the branch of another tree and ran to the next. Babri followed the leaping Squirrel until it arrived at a tree crammed with nuts.

"Why do you take nuts into the trees when so many cover the jungle floor?" asked the why child.

"Nuts plentiful today are not always so," answered Squirrel. "We store them when we can to have food during times of shortage, which always come. That is the way of things for squirrels."

Satisfied, Babri took the nut Squirrel offered him and chewed it, but the flavor did not suit the young tiger.

*N*ow Babri was deep into the jungle, but he thought he still could see the fern glade. Then he heard something like faint music behind him. He turned and walked slowly toward it but could not locate the sound, though it was still in his ears. Finally, Babri realized the music was coming from above. Climbing the tree next to him, he saw a tangle of twigs shaped like a dish. Inside nestled a small bird like none he knew.

"Why are you alone?" asked the why child.

"Because my mother has gone to find me food," trilled Bird.

"Why do you make sounds like music?"

"To help her find me again. That is the way of things for birds."

Mothers finding children is also the way of things for tigers, thought Babri, who wanted to be with his mother right now! He climbed down and started for home. But Babri did not know which way to go.

*B*abri needed help but could find no one except Frog. Grabbing him, Babri asked, "How do I get to the fern glade at the edge of the jungle?"

"I do not know because I never travel. But my cousin Fish holds the secrets of the world," explained Frog. "All water is one water, and the earth's knowledge washes down rivulets and streams to lodge in his gills. He can tell you."

*B*abri plunged into the stream, right into a school of fish. Seizing one, he asked, "How do I get to the fern glade at the edge of the jungle?"

"Not now," said Fish. "We are grieving because cantankerous and proud Turtle just snatched away our sister."

"If your sister is returned, will you then tell me?" asked the why child.

"Immediately," was the reply. "That is the way of things with fish."

*T*urtle was easy to find. Fast in water but slow on land, he had not traveled far. The eager tiger tried to grab the fish from Turtle's mouth, but Turtle bit down harder. Babri released his grip on the fish and thought for a moment about what he should do. Then he spoke.

"Frog told me you never eat fresh fish."

"M-m-m-m-m-p-h," replied Turtle.

"He said you always eat old fish cast aside by other animals because you are too dull and slow to catch your own."

Turtle could not bear this insult. "I do not eat old fish!" he screeched. "I catch fresh ones whenever I want."

At Turtle's first word, the fish fell to the ground, was scooped up by Babri and returned to the stream before Turtle could finish speaking.

Fish kept his promise. "Find Elephant and he will take you home." Fish then put the message in the water so Elephant would know.

Where do I find Elephant? wondered Babri and began walking.

You seem sad, young tiger. May I help?" asked a smooth voice coming from someone Babri could not see. He hoped it was Elephant.

"Yes. I want to go to my mother in the fern glade at the edge of the jungle," said Babri as his eyes searched the bushes and trees for Elephant.

"You're in luck," said the voice. "Simply climb on my back and I'll give you a ride there." At that moment Crocodile slithered into view, his huge tongue caressing rows of pointed teeth. Babri did not like what he saw and leaped up a tree.

"No ride? No matter," said Crocodile. "I'll stay right here until you get hungry enough to come down."

Babri was hungry right now. He watched the sun set and stared as the moon rose. Feeling the cool night air descend, he missed his mother more than ever. How could he get out of this tree to find her?

Just before dawn, the answer came: Squirrel had run from tree to tree, and he could do the same. Slowly and quietly Babri crawled out to the end of the branch and pulled himself over to the next tree. Crocodile did not move. Quickly Babri advanced to another tree, and then another. Faster now, he jumped to the branch of a new tree—and felt it sag.

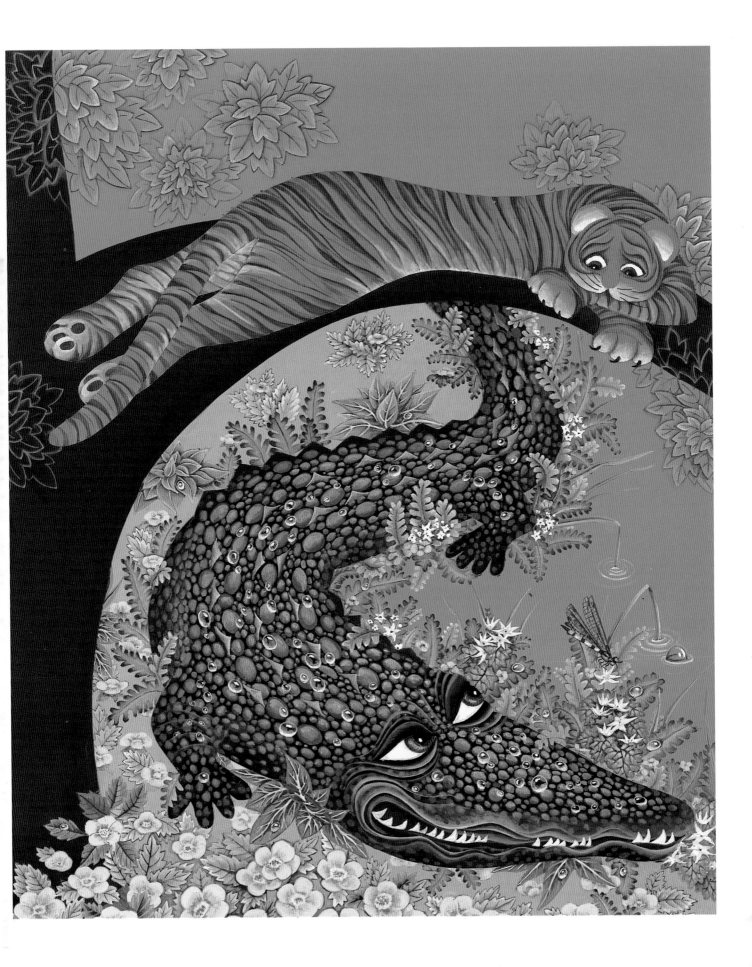

W hat is-s-s-s this-s-s-s?" A head appeared above Babri, weaving back and forth on a long neck. "How nic-c-c-c-e to s-s-s-ee you, little cherub."

Babri froze. Dangling from Snake, he felt sweat run down his back.

"You pay me a vis-s-s-s-it, my dumpling? I hope you can s-s-s-stay for dinner."

Babri let go and dropped to the ground. Branches stinging his face, he dashed blindly through the underbrush, smacked headlong into a tree trunk, tangled himself in vines, and tumbled into a small stream. He ran and ran until he could run no more. He did not know where he was and did not know how to find Elephant. He wanted something to eat. But he wanted nothing more than his mother.

Then the ground under him began to move.

Snake!" Babri shrieked as he was raised into the air so high he grabbed a tree limb to balance himself. He then discovered the snake was Elephant's trunk and noticed the kind brown eyes. He spied the sharp tusks, solid enough to pierce Crocodile's armor hide. He looked down at the massive flat feet which could make short work of Snake.

"Fish gave me the message, young Babri, but all your running made my work difficult," said Elephant. "Now I have you, though. Next stop—fern glade at the edge of the jungle."

Babri hugged the great gray nose all the way home.

*E*lephant arrived at the fern glade by midmorning, waking the owls with his heavy footsteps. Babri's mother was not there. Elephant asked Owl what he knew.

"She left in a hurry yesterday afternoon, calling Babri's name," said Owl. "During the hunt last night, I saw her deep in the jungle. More, I cannot say."

As Elephant pondered this and Babri began to worry, Baby Owl hooted, "Look down the trail! She's coming back!"

Seeing Babri, his mother sprang to him, gathered him up, and buried him in a blanket of licks. "My lost child, whom I love more than air, are you truly safe?" As she nuzzled and hugged Babri, he told his story. She gave him food as she listened.

"Do you know of Turtle and Crocodile and Snake who hangs in a tree?" asked Babri between bites.

"Yes, my joy child."

"How?" asked Babri.

"I am older than you and have seen more of the world."

"Did you know I would return safely?"

"I did not know you would return safely, but I hoped you would and searched for you without stopping. Now you are back, and we are together. And that is the way of things," she purred.

Satisfied, Babri snuggled close and shut his eyes, both of them, awaiting a delicious nap.

Babri

Illustrated by Fahimeh Amiri
using her unique composition
of watercolor applied over paper collage

Edited by Linda Nimori

Designed by Mary Ellen Thompson
with display lines in Letraset® Malibu™
and body text in Adobe® Optima

Printed and bound in China by Leefung / Asco Printers, Ltd.